LEGO friends

The
Superstar Concert

PUFFIN

PUFFIN BOOKS

Published by the Penguin Group
Penguin Books Ltd, 80 Strand, London WC2R 0RL, England
Penguin Group (USA) Inc., 375 Hudson Street, New York, New York 10014, USA
Penguin Group (Canada), 90 Eglinton Avenue East, Suite 700, Toronto, Ontario, Canada M4P 2Y3
(a division of Pearson Penguin Canada Inc.)
Penguin Ireland, 25 St Stephen's Green, Dublin 2, Ireland (a division of Penguin Books Ltd)
Penguin Group (Australia), 707 Collins Street, Melbourne, Victoria 3008, Australia
(a division of Pearson Australia Group Pty Ltd)
Penguin Books India Pvt Ltd, 11 Community Centre, Panchsheel Park, New Delhi – 110 017, India
Penguin Group (NZ), 67 Apollo Drive, Rosedale, Auckland 0632, New Zealand
(a division of Pearson New Zealand Ltd)
Penguin Books (South Africa) (Pty) Ltd, Block D, Rosebank Office Park, 181 Jan Smuts Avenue, Parktown
North, Gauteng 2193, South Africa

Penguin Books Ltd, Registered Offices: 80 Strand, London WC2R 0RL, England

puffinbooks.com

First published 2013
001

Written by Poppy Bloom
Illustrations by AMEET Studio Sp. z o.o.
Text and illustrations copyright © AMEET Sp. z o.o., 2013

Produced by AMEET Sp. ż o.o. under license from the LEGO Group.

AMEET Sp. z o.o.
Nowe Sady 6, 94-102 Łódź – Poland
ameet@ameet.com.pl   www.ameet.pl

LEGO, the LEGO logo and the Brick and Knob configurations
are trademarks of the LEGO Group.
©2013 The LEGO Group.

Set in Bembo.
Printed in Poland by AMEET Sp. z o.o.

British Library Cataloguing in Publication Data
A CIP catalogue record for this book is available from the British Library

ISBN: 978-0-72327-978-5

Item name: LEGO® Friends. The Superstar Concert
Series: LBW
Item number: LBW-101
Batch: 01

The Superstar Concert

Poppy Bloom

Andrea
Star Performer

Mia
Animal Lover

Olivia
Brilliant
Inventor

Stephanie
Social Butterfly

Emma
Stylish Designer

Chelsea
Uptown Girl

Piper Page
The greatest
pop star ever!

Contents

1
Exciting News

Andrea stepped up to the microphone and ran a hand through her curly dark hair. For just a moment she imagined she was onstage in a huge stadium with a band behind her, preparing to perform for thousands of screaming fans.

"Go, Andrea!" someone shouted.

She squinted against the glow of the spotlight. Stephanie, one of her best friends, was out there in the audience clapping and grinning, her blonde head nodding with excitement. Their other best friends Mia,

Emma, and Olivia, were crammed into the booth with Stephanie.

Seeing her friends brought Andrea back to reality. It was the Summer Karaoke Night at the café, not a superstar sell-out concert. Instead of thousands of screaming fans in a giant stadium, she was singing for thirty residents of Heartlake City, seated at the café's familiar bright red tables and cosy seating booths.

But that was okay. Andrea loved the Summer Karaoke Night. It gave her a chance to do her favourite thing in the world – perform!

"I think I'll sing one of my favourites tonight," she announced with a smile. "'Friends Forever' by Piper Page."

"Good one!" Emma called out.

Marie, the owner of the café, nodded and hit a button on the karaoke machine. The opening notes of 'Friends Forever' boomed out of the speakers.

Andrea swayed to the music, her sparkly green skirt shimmering in the light. Then she took the microphone.

"We were strangers when we met," she sang. "Now we're close as friends can get . . ."

Her voice rang out through the speakers, clear and strong. All around the café, people started tapping their feet. Halfway through, almost the entire audience was singing along to the catchy, familiar chorus:

"We're friends forever, friends forever –
We're stuck like glue, me and you.
Friends, friends, friends, forever true!"

The whole café erupted into cheers as the song ended. Andrea took a bow.

"Thank you!" she cried. "You've been a brilliant audience!"

She wished she could stay onstage, but the next performer was already racing over to grab the microphone. It was Jacob, a boy from her class at school.

"'Thanks for being my opening act,
Andrea," he said with a grin. Jacob was always
joking around.

"You're welcome," Andrea said with a smile.
"Knock 'em dead."

She hurried over to her friends. When she
reached their booth, Stephanie leapt up and
hugged her.

"That was amazing, Andrea!" Stephanie exclaimed. "You sounded just like Piper Page. No, even better!"

"I doubt that." Andrea laughed and hugged her back. Then she slid into the empty seat beside Olivia. "But thanks."

"Piper Page is the best singer ever, isn't she?" Emma said, twirling a lock of black hair between her fingers.

"Definitely!" Stephanie sat down and reached for her drink. "Did you guys know that Piper is from Heartlake City? She was discovered when she wasn't much older than we are now."

"I know," Mia said. "I heard her whole family still lives here."

"Really?" Olivia's brown eyes sparkled. She'd moved to town recently, so she didn't know as much about Heartlake City as her friends.

"Where do they live?"

"Over by Heartlake Harbour, I think."
Stephanie sipped her drink. "Her parents used to
run one of the seafood restaurants over there."

"They probably don't have to work at all
these days," Emma guessed. "Piper's super
rich! Her last album went platinum on the
day it was released."

"It's amazing that she grew up and was
discovered right here where we all live,"
Olivia said.

"It's amazing, but not surprising," Stephanie
grinned. "Heartlake City is full of talented
people. Like us! Mia's amazing with animals,
Emma does beautiful makeovers, Olivia is a
genius inventor –"

"You throw the best parties!" Emma offered.
Stephanie smiled and continued. "Last

but not least, we have our very own singing superstar-in-the-making, Andrea!"

Andrea grinned and looked at the stage. Jacob was singing a loud but off-key version of a popular song.

"Yeah, Heartlake City is full of talented people," she agreed. "But not all of them are talented at singing!"

Stephanie, Emma, and Olivia laughed. They all knew Jacob was a good sport. He wouldn't mind them making a joke.

"Uh oh, look who's here," Mia said quietly.

The others turned to look. A girl their age had just walked in. She had wavy blonde hair, brown eyes and a snooty look.

"Ugh, it's Chelsea Noble," Stephanie whispered.

The five girls went to school with Chelsea.

They all tried to be nice to her, but sometimes it wasn't easy. She was bossy and stuck-up and loved to gossip. She also liked to boast about her expensive clothes, like the trendy floral top and designer jeans she was wearing now.

Jacob's song was almost finished. Chelsea marched up to the edge of the stage. "I'm next!" she told Marie loudly.

"Shh!" the café owner hushed her. "You're interrupting Jacob's song."

Jacob heard them and stopped singing. "It's OK," he said with a grin. "I'm surprised nobody interrupted me before this."

That made everyone laugh, including Andrea and her friends. "Encore! Encore!" Stephanie shouted.

"No encores! It's my turn." Chelsea climbed

on to the stage and grabbed the microphone from Jacob. "I'm ready," she said. "I'm going to sing 'Friends Forever' by Piper Page."

"Are you sure?" Marie asked. "Another singer did that one a few minutes ago."

Chelsea frowned. "I don't care. There's no rule that says I can't do it, is there?"

"I suppose not," Marie said with a shrug. "Off you go, then . . ."

She started the karaoke machine. Chelsea closed her eyes and swayed as the music started.

"She's acting even weirder than usual," Stephanie whispered to her friends. "Why do you think she's so determined to do that song?"

"I have no idea," Olivia said. "But I'm sure she'd think twice if she knew that Andrea had just sang it."

"Shh," Andrea warned. "We shouldn't talk during her performance."

Even though Andrea didn't like Chelsea very much, she didn't want to be rude. She sipped her water and listened to the song. Chelsea's voice was a little weak, and she fluffed some of the high notes. But overall, it wasn't too bad. At the end, everyone in the café applauded politely.

Chelsea left the stage and strolled past the booth. "Nicely done, Chelsea!" Andrea called out.

Chelsea stopped. "Thanks," she said, sounding smug. "I suppose you've guessed why I'm here tonight practising that song."

"No." Andrea traded a glance with her friends, who looked as mystified as she felt. "Why?"

"You mean you haven't heard?" Chelsea said. "Piper Page is coming back to Heartlake City!"

2
Summer Sleepover

"What?" Olivia gasped. "Piper Page is coming here?"

"When?" Andrea exclaimed.

"Why?" Stephanie added.

Chelsea looked pleased to be the one in the know. "I'm surprised you haven't heard about it, Stephanie," she said. "I thought you knew about everything that happened around town. And Olivia, doesn't your father work for the newspaper? I can't believe he didn't tell you about the big news."

"Just tell us!" Emma cried.

"All right," Chelsea said. "Piper Page started this charity . . ."

"Page's Pets," Mia cut in quickly. "It's a charity that helps to find homes for homeless animals."

"That's the one, I guess," Chelsea said with a shrug. "Anyway, Piper's coming back to Heartlake City to put on a fundraiser. It's an exclusive concert."

"Wow!" Olivia said. "A Piper Page concert right here in Heartlake City? That's amazing!"

"Wait, that's not even the coolest part. You see, it's not going to be just any concert," Chelsea went on. "It's going to take place on a yacht!"

Emma blinked, looking confused. "A concert on a boat?"

Chelsea rolled her eyes. "It's not just a boat. It's a huge yacht! It's even bigger than my family's yacht."

"Wow," Andrea said. Chelsea's family was one of the richest in Heartlake City. Andrea and her friends had seen Chelsea riding around on her family's yacht lots of times.

"Piper's yacht is brand new and top of the range," Chelsea went on. "I know that for a fact, because it's moored a few places down from ours."

"Piper won't be able to fit many people on a yacht," Stephanie said dubiously. "Not even a big one. I wonder why she didn't decide to have the concert at the stadium or the park. She'd have room for lots more fans that way. And more fans means more money for the charity."

Andrea laughed. "Maybe you should volunteer to organize the fundraiser for her, Steph."

"Maybe I should!"
Stephanie said with
a grin.

Chelsea looked
annoyed.

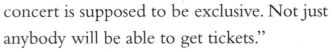

"I doubt Piper
needs your help.
And I told you, this
concert is supposed to be exclusive. Not just
anybody will be able to get tickets."

Olivia looked worried. "But I want to go!
It would be great to get a closer look at that
yacht with all that sophisticated technology
on board."

Chelsea shrugged. "Don't worry. If you guys
can't get tickets, I'll be sure to tell you all about
the concert afterwards." With that, she spun on
her heel and hurried out of the café.

Later that evening, the five friends were having a sleepover. It was a beautiful summer night, so they'd decided to camp out under the stars in Olivia's tree house. They'd changed into their pyjamas, made a big bowl of popcorn, and crawled into their sleeping bags amid a pile of comfy pillows. Olivia's dog, Scarlett, was snuggled between Olivia and Mia. A Piper Page song was playing softly through Andrea's portable speakers.

"I still can't believe Piper Page is coming to town!" Andrea hugged her pillow.

"This is so exciting," Emma said. "We have to decide what we're going to wear on the yacht."

"First we have to figure out how to get tickets," Mia reminded her, scratching Scarlett behind the ears.

Emma tossed a piece of popcorn into her mouth. She looked as stylish as ever in lace-trimmed pyjamas. "I'll leave that part to you guys. My job is planning our outfits."

"Good plan." Stephanie said. "That way we're sure to be the best-dressed fans on the yacht. Piper will probably come over and ask us for fashion tips!"

Olivia was humming along with the music. "At least now we know why Chelsea wanted to practise singing 'Friends Forever' tonight," she said.

"We do?" Emma looked confused.

Andrea nodded. "Whenever Piper sings 'Friends Forever' in concert, she always sends an assistant into the audience with a microphone so fans can help her sing the chorus."

"You could be one of those fans, Andrea!"
Stephanie said.

"Definitely!" Andrea jumped to her feet,
smoothed down her purple nightgown and
belted out a few lines of the song that
was playing.

Emma applauded. "That was great!" she cried.
"I bet Piper would love your voice, Andrea."

"I know she would," Stephanie agreed.
"Who knows, she might even help Andrea
to launch her own singing career."

Andrea flopped back down onto her
sleeping bag. "That would be a dream come
true!" she exclaimed. "Now we really have to
make sure we get tickets to that concert."

"But how?" Mia said, tying her red hair
up in a ponytail. "If the concert is really on a
yacht, only a few people will be able to go."

"Don't panic." Stephanie took another handful of popcorn. "We don't even know how the tickets will be allocated yet. Let's go down to the town hall first thing tomorrow and find out."

"Good idea." Andrea closed her eyes, picturing herself singing the chorus of 'Friends Forever' with Piper Page. "We've got to figure out a way to be there – no matter what!"

3
A Little Competition

The next morning, Andrea yawned and opened one eye. Bright sunlight was streaming in through the gap in the sheet they'd strung up over the tree house. When Andrea looked around, she saw that all her friends were still asleep.

"Rise and shine, everyone!" Andrea sang out, kicking her way out of her sleeping bag. She jumped to her feet and nudged Emma with her toe. "It's morning!"

Emma moaned and turned over. "Morning? I don't believe it," she mumbled. "I only fell asleep five minutes ago."

Mia sat up and stretched. "It feels that way, doesn't it?" she said. "We did stay up awfully late."

"Yeah," Andrea said with a smile. They'd stayed awake until well past midnight, eating popcorn and singing along to every Piper Page song at least three times. "It was fun."

"Are you awake, Steph?" Mia rolled over and poked her friend.

"Sort of," Stephanie said without opening her eyes.

Just then Scarlett barked at the foot of the tree.

"Good morning, Scarlett!" Olivia smiled down at her dog. Then she turned to her friends. "Does anyone else smell pancakes?"

"Pancakes?" Stephanie opened her eyes and sat up immediately. "Yum! What are you lazybones waiting for? Let's get going!"

A few minutes later, the five girls entered Olivia's sunny green-and-white kitchen. Olivia's father was at the cooker with a spatula in his hand and several pancakes sizzling on the griddle.

"Good morning, girls," he said with a smile. "I was just wondering if I was going to have to eat all these pancakes myself." He gestured towards a plate on the kitchen worktop nearby. It was piled high with beautiful golden pancakes.

"Wow!" Stephanie hurried over to grab the plate. "These look delicious."

"Thanks, Dad." Olivia gave him a kiss on the cheek before joining her friends at the table.

"It's going to be another beautiful summer day," Olivia's dad said as he flipped a pancake.

"What are you girls doing today? You could go to the beach, or the swimming baths?"

"We might do that later." Andrea drizzled syrup over her pancakes. "First we have to go to the town hall."

Olivia's dad looked surprised. "The town hall? Why do you need to go there?"

"We've heard that Piper Page is coming to town," Olivia began. She and her friends took turns telling her dad what they knew about the concert.

"Oh right, I heard about that," he said when they'd finished. "The mayor thinks that the event will raise a lot of money for the charity."

"Do you know how many tickets there will be, Dad?" Olivia asked. "Or how they're going to decide who gets the tickets?"

"Sorry, I'm afraid not." He used the spatula to slide a pancake from the griddle. "I just heard a couple of the reporters at work talking about it. But I'm sure you'll be able to find out all the details at the town hall."

As soon as they finished breakfast, the five girls walked into town. It was a lovely day,

and lots of people were wandering around the old cobblestoned town square. Just outside the town hall, the girls spotted a familiar face.

"Chelsea!" Olivia blurted out. "What are you doing here?"

"Oh, hi." Chelsea didn't seem very happy to see them, either. "I came to find out when the tickets are going on sale for the Piper Page concert. My dad gave me a load of money and said that I can buy as many tickets as I like."

"We came to find out about tickets, too." Emma sounded worried. "But we didn't bring any money."

"Never mind," Stephanie said. "Let's just get inside and ask about the tickets, OK?"

As the girls entered the town hall foyer with Chelsea trailing behind, they spotted another familiar face. It was the mayor. He was striding across the floor towards them, looking as dapper as ever in a pinstripe suit.

"Good morning, girls," he said, rubbing his beard. "What brings you to the town hall on this lovely summer day?"

"We came to find out about the Piper Page concert," Andrea said eagerly.

"Ah, yes." The mayor puffed out his chest and smiled. "That's going to be quite an event. Good publicity for Heartlake City!"

"Do you know when the tickets are going on sale?" Chelsea asked.

"Oh, I'm afraid you can't buy tickets," the mayor said.

Andrea's heart sank. "We can't? Oh, no – are the tickets sold out already?"

"No, no, nothing like that." The mayor chuckled. "You see, Piper Page wants this to be a true charity event.

36

I was just on my way over to the radio station to make an announcement about it and there will be a notice on the Heartlake City website as well."

"A true charity event? What does that mean?" Mia asked.

"It means Piper is asking all of her local fans to raise as much money for Page's Pets as they can," the mayor explained. "The twenty-five people who make the most for the charity by the end of the week will receive tickets to the yacht concert."

Olivia gasped. "What a great idea!"

"What a stupid idea!" Chelsea exclaimed at the same time. When the mayor shot her a surprised look, she frowned. "I mean, uh, what an interesting idea," she muttered.

Andrea swallowed a laugh. All of them knew that Chelsea didn't like working hard at

anything. And she wasn't very interested in charity.

On the other hand, Andrea and her friends loved helping charities. They were sure to win five of those tickets!

"Thanks for the information, sir," Stephanie said. "We'd better get straight to work!"

4
Making Plans

"Did you see the look on Chelsea's face when she heard the only way to get tickets is by doing charity work?" Emma giggled as the five friends left City Hall. "I thought she was going to explode!"

"Never mind her," Olivia said. "What are we going to do to raise money for Page's Pets?"

"I know what I want to do," Mia said. "You guys know Joanna, right?"

Stephanie nodded. "You mean the lady who runs the Heartlake Pet Salon? What about her?"

"She's taking this week off for a trip to Clearspring Mountains," Mia said. "She was going to close the salon while she's away. But I could volunteer to take it over! Then I could groom the pets that come in, and donate all of the money I make to Piper Page's charity."

"Great idea," Stephanie said. "You're fantastic with animals, Mia. Plus, it's extra cool because you'll be helping them in two ways – grooming, and also raising money for an animal charity. You're sure to win a ticket to that concert!"

"I hope so," Mia smiled. "But it won't be any fun if you guys aren't there, too. What are you going to do to raise money?"

"There's some really nice animal-print fabric for sale in the second-hand shop," Emma said. "I could make hairbands and bows out of it.

Then I can sell them at the farmer's market."

"That sounds great," Mia said. "I'll definitely buy one."

"Me too," Stephanie said. "If Emma makes them, they're sure to be the most fashionable new accessory in Heartlake City!"

"Plus it has an animal theme, just like Mia's plan." Olivia smiled.

"Our work doesn't have to have an animal theme, does it?" Stephanie sounded worried. "Because I was thinking I could bake cupcakes and sell them."

"Brilliant," Andrea said. "Your cupcakes are delicious, Steph! Maybe you could use icing to decorate some of them with pictures of animals?"

"Perfect!" Emma clapped her hands. "What about you two?" She smiled at Andrea and Olivia.

"I'm not sure," Andrea said.

Olivia was looking at something further down the street. "Hang on a second," she said. "It looks like that lady is having trouble with her bike."

The other girls turned to look. A young woman was kneeling beside a bicycle, looking worried.

"Is everything okay?" Olivia asked, walking over to her.

The woman looked up. "I don't think so," she said. "My brakes aren't working properly."

"Can I take a look?" Olivia reached for the bicycle.

"Don't worry, Olivia can fix anything,"

Andrea reassured the woman.

"I guess I'm lucky I ran into her, then," she replied with a smile.

Moments later, the bicycle was fixed. Olivia hopped on and rode in a circle to test it.

"That should do it," she said, stopping in front of the bicycle's owner. "Happy pedalling."

"Wow!" The woman took the bicycle from her. "I thought I was going to have to take it to the repair shop. How can I ever thank you?"

"I know a way," Stephanie said before Olivia could respond. "You could make a donation to Page's Pets. That's a charity that helps animals. We're trying to raise money for it."

"I've heard of that charity," the woman said. "I'd be happy to donate to it." She reached into her pocket for some change. "Good luck – and thanks again!"

She cycled away, ringing her bicycle bell as she went. Olivia stared at the money in her hand. "Wow, I guess I'm off to a good start," she said. "It's a pity I can't make enough money just by fixing bikes."

"You could fix other things too," Stephanie said. "Like people's mobile phones, or toasters,

and other things that aren't working properly."

"Great idea," Andrea said. "Now help me to figure out what I can do to raise money for Page's Pets."

"Isn't it obvious?" Stephanie said. "We're all using our special talents to raise money. Mia is great with animals, so she's grooming pets."

"And Olivia can fix anything, so she's doing that," Mia said.

"Emma is the most fashionable person I know," Olivia added. "Her hairbands and bows are sure to be a big hit."

"Don't forget Stephanie's delicious cupcakes." Emma licked her lips. "She's a fantastic baker."

"I get it," Andrea said. "I guess my biggest talent is singing. Well, that and acting. And of course dancing, and composing songs, and . . ."

"Exactly!" Stephanie interrupted. "People would definitely pay money to listen to you sing."

"And if you sing songs about animals, you'll even fit the theme!" Olivia added with a laugh.

Andrea grinned. "You guys are geniuses. I'll do it!"

"Great." Stephanie stuck out her hand. "Here's to all of us raising lots of money for Page's Pets – and getting to watch Andrea sing 'Friends Forever' with Piper Page!"

The other four girls put their hands on top of Stephanie's. "Friends forever!" Stephanie cried.

"Friends forever!" the others shouted.

Andrea dropped her hand, eager to get started. "We only have until the end of the week," she reminded the others. "There's no time to waste."

"That's true," Mia said. "So what are we waiting for? Let's go and help some homeless pets!"

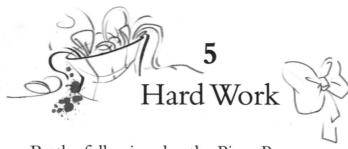

5
Hard Work

By the following day, the Piper Page
fundraising effort was the talk of Heartlake
City. The mayor had made his announcement
on the radio, the evening news had done a
story, and many local businesses had signs in
their windows.

"Thanks for helping me, Andrea," Emma
said as the two girls arrived at the local
farmer's market. "I never could have carried all
these things myself."

"You're welcome." Andrea tightened her
grip on the box she was carrying. "I can't

believe you made so many bows and hairbands in such a short time."

"It was fun." Emma put her box on an empty table. "When the owner of the shop heard what I was doing, she donated all the fabric for free."

"Cool." Andrea placed her box beside Emma's. "I guess I'd better get to work, too. I'm going to put on a fabulous fundraising concert in the park."

"Good luck!" Emma called as Andrea hurried off. "I'm sure it'll be a big success!"

Andrea went home and changed into a sparkly silver top and her favourite pink skirt. She packed her microphone and mini speakers into her bag. Then she took the jar that Olivia had helped her to decorate the night before with pictures of pets and a few words about Piper's charity. Andrea hoped it would be big enough to hold all of her donations!

She hurried to the park and set up her
equipment in a pretty spot near the fountain.
There weren't many people nearby – just a few
older couples feeding the squirrels and a family
with young children having a picnic on the
grass. But Andrea was sure more people would
show up when they heard the music.
She cleared her throat, turned on the
microphone, and began to sing.

She started with a children's song about
a farmer with lots of animals. A handful of
small children wandered over and to watch.
One even sang along for a while.

When the song was over, Andrea smiled at
the children. "I'm singing for charity today,"
she told them. "Do you have any money to
donate? If you do, you can drop it into my
collection jar."

Most of the children just stared at her. Then
one little boy plucked a few blades of grass and
dropped them into the jar.

"Wait – no!" Andrea grabbed the jar, tipped
the grass out, and set it back on the ground.
"This is for donations only, OK? I'm trying to
help homeless animals."

"What do you mean?" A little girl's lower lip
trembled. "Why are the animals homeless?"

"They just are." Andrea said.

"I don't know any homeless animals," said another child. "My dog lives in a kennel."

"My cat lives on my bed," a girl spoke up. "Except when she lives on my brother's bed. Is she homeless?"

"No – but listen, would you like to hear me sing another song?"

Halfway through her next song, some of the children wandered off. As she finished, a woman came and took the hand of a small boy.

"Excuse me," Andrea said. "I'm singing to raise money for Page's Pets. That's a charity that tries to–"

"Sounds lovely," the woman muttered, sounding distracted. She pulled a couple of coins out of her pocket and tossed them into the jar. Then she pulled her child away.

Andrea looked at the coins.
It wasn't even enough money to buy
a pack of chewing gum! At this rate,
it would take forever to raise enough
to earn a place on the yacht.

Thinking about the yacht – and
the chance to sing for Piper Page –
gave her new determination. She started
another song, and then another. Some of the
children left, while others arrived to take their
places. A few adults wandered over to listen.
But only a couple of them put money in the
collection jar.

As Andrea was singing a song about a
monkey, she spotted Stephanie walking
towards her. At the end of the song, Stephanie
dropped some money in Andrea's jar and then
applauded loudly.

"How's the concert going?" she asked.

"Great," Andrea said. "But there doesn't seem to be enough people around to make a real audience. Where is everybody? The park should be packed on a gorgeous day like this."

Stephanie glanced around. "It is pretty hot today – I bet everyone's at the beach."

"You're probably right," Andrea said. "Hey, what are you doing here, anyway? Shouldn't you be baking cupcakes?"

Stephanie checked her watch. "The latest batch just went into the oven," she said. "Mum's keeping an eye on them. I decided to check on how the rest of you are doing while they're cooking."

"Did you go to the farmer's market to see Emma?" Andrea asked.

Stephanie nodded. "I could hardly get near

her table. Her hairbands and bows are a big hit. I've already seen a few people walking around wearing them."

"That's great! At this rate, she'll earn a ticket to the yacht by the end of the day," Andrea said with a smile.

She crossed her fingers. If only she could say the same!

That afternoon, the five girls met at the café to compare notes. Andrea was the first to arrive, so she ordered drinks for everyone. When Stephanie hurried in, she had flour on her rosy cheeks. Olivia's hands were stained with axle grease. Emma had strands of brightly coloured fabric stuck in her long black hair. Mia was covered in dog and cat hair from head to toe.

But all of them looked happy. "What a great day!" Emma sang out. "It seems like everyone in Heartlake City wants to help homeless pets."

Stephanie nodded and sipped her drink. "My cupcakes sold out in less than an hour. I had to bake three more batches!"

"I could barely keep up with all of the pets that needed to be groomed," Mia added, picking a clump of fluffy white fur off her blue tank top.

"And I fixed two bikes, a vacuum cleaner, and my dad's coffee maker. Plus my neighbour paid me a lot of money for helping him to set up his new smartphone." Olivia turned to smile at Andrea. "What about you? I bet your concert was a big hit."

"Not exactly," Andrea said. "There weren't many people at the park today, so I didn't make much money. Definitely not enough to get me on the yacht."

Olivia looked alarmed. "You have to get a ticket!"

"I know." Andrea shrugged. "But don't worry, I'm not giving up."

"That's the spirit!" said Emma. "If people will pay money to hear Piper Page sing, they'll pay to hear you, too!"

"Thanks, Emma. I think I just need a better location," Andrea mused.

Mia looked thoughtful. "You need to find a spot where people who care about animals gather. Like the veterinary clinic."

"How about the pet shop on Fountain Street?" Olivia suggested. "There are always lots of customers in there."

"And they're already there to spend money on animals," Stephanie finished. "Brilliant idea, Olivia!"

"Definitely." Andrea smiled, excited by the new plan. "I'll go down first thing tomorrow and see if they'll let me put on a show there!"

6

The Show Must Go On

Pauline, the little old lady who owned
Pauline's Pet Pantry, listened carefully as Andrea
outlined her plan.

"Page's Pets, eh?" Pauline said, looking at
Andrea over her glasses. "I know all about
them. That group has helped a lot of animals.
Of course you're welcome to fundraise for
them here."

"Great! Thanks a lot." Andrea glanced
around the shop. There wasn't much room, the
shelves were overflowing with pet food, pet
toys, and other products. "Where do you want
me to set up?"

"How about over there by the pet beds?" Pauline pointed to an open area in the middle of the shop.

"OK. I'll go and get ready to start." Andrea quickly set up her speakers and put the collection jar on a table.

Donation charity concert

There were already several customers in the shop. One was Jacob, the boy from school. He wandered over when he spotted her.

"Hi, Andrea," he said. He noticed the sign on the collection jar. "Are you trying to win a place on the Piper Page yacht?"

"Yes. Would you like to make a donation?"
Andrea pointed to her jar.

"Sure." Jacob reached into his pocket and
pulled out a few coins. "But I can only afford a
small donation. I need the rest of my money to
buy a birthday present for my sister."

"It's OK – every little bit helps," Andrea said.
"What are you going to buy for your sister?"

"I'm not sure." Jacob glanced around the
shop. "She loves animals, so I came here. But
I can't see anything that would make a good
birthday present."

Suddenly Andrea had an idea. "Emma is
selling some really nice handmade hair bows
over at the farmer's market today," she said.
"They have animals on them. Maybe your
sister would like one."

Jacob's eyes lit up. "That sounds perfect!" he

exclaimed. "She loves stuff like that. Thanks for the idea!"

As Jacob rushed out, Andrea noticed two women standing near the dog treats. She grabbed her microphone and started singing a cheerful song about a happy puppy. One of the women smiled and tapped her foot along with the beat. But neither of them came any closer.

Andrea kept singing. A few people dropped coins into her jar. But most of the customers just wandered past with their cat toys or bags of dog food.

After a while, Pauline came over to give Andrea a bottle of water. "I thought you might need this," she said. "You've been singing non-stop for over half an hour."

"Thanks." Andrea took a drink of water. "I needed that."

"Sorry it's not very cold," the woman said. "I have a mini fridge in the back room, but it stopped working last week."

"Really? My friend Olivia might be able to fix it for you," Andrea said. She explained about Olivia's fundraising project.

"Wonderful!" Pauline said. "What's her phone number? I'll call her right away."

Andrea gave her the number. Then she finished the water and went back to singing.

An hour later, Andrea was just finishing a song when the door flew open. A man rushed in with a large poodle on a lead. At least Andrea thought it was a poodle. It was difficult to tell, since the dog was covered in mud, twigs, and leaves from head to toe. He even had a pine cone stuck in his curly topknot.

Andrea was so surprised by the sight that she stopped singing.

"Help!" the man cried, heading straight for the counter. "I need a really good brush. Or some strong dog shampoo. Or something."

He waved helplessly at the dog, who sat down to scratch. Dirt flew everywhere as the dog pawed at his neck.

"Oh, dear." Pauline leaned over the counter for a better look at the dirty dog. "It's going to take a lot of shampoo to clean up this fellow! Unfortunately, I'm almost sold out."

"Oh, no." The man looked anxious. "But I need to get him clean before I meet my girlfriend for lunch! It's her dog, and she'll kill me if she sees him looking like this. Please – I'll pay anything!"

"I've got an idea." Andrea hurried over. "My friend is grooming dogs today over at the pet salon. She can get your girlfriend's dog cleaned up, no problem. And all of the money goes to a fantastic animal charity."

"That sounds great." The man looked relieved. "Where's the salon?"

Andrea gave him directions. The man thanked her, then hurried out of the shop with the muddy dog trotting beside him.

"Thanks for the suggestion, Andrea," Pauline said. "I hope your friend is up for some hard work!"

Andrea laughed. "She'll love it," she assured
Pauline. "Now I'd better get back to
work myself."

Five or six songs later, Andrea saw Olivia walking
into the pet shop. She was holding a cupcake
with a cute parrot painted on it in icing.

"How's it going?" Olivia asked Andrea. "You
sound great!"

"Thanks." Andrea looked into collection jar.
"I'm having fun, and people seem to like the
music. But I'm still not making much money."

"Never mind." Olivia looked sympathetic.
"Here, I brought you this cupcake. I just
managed to grab it before Steph's latest batch
sold out."

"Yum! Thanks." Andrea accepted the
cupcake eagerly.

Pauline came over. "What a lovely cupcake," she said. "Where did you get it?"

Andrea and Olivia explained about Stephanie's fundraiser. "She's a fantastic baker," Andrea added. "All her stuff is delicious."

"Does she do special orders?" Pauline asked. "I'm throwing a dinner party tomorrow night, and I'd love to serve something like that."

"I'm sure Stephanie would be happy to make you some special cupcakes," Andrea said. "I can give you her number if you like."

Soon, Pauline was hurrying off to call Stephanie.

"I'd better go and take a look at that broken fridge," Olivia said. "Thanks for telling Pauline about me."

"You're welcome." Andrea smiled and waved as Olivia headed for the back room. She liked nothing better than helping her friends.

Then she looked into her collection jar again and sighed. There were still only a couple of notes and some coins in there.

"I guess it's true what they say," she muttered with a sad smile. "It's not easy making a living in show business."

Then she took a deep breath and started to sing again.

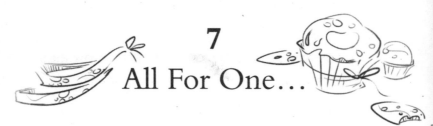

7
All For One...

The next morning, the girls met at Olivia's tree house. "How did everyone do yesterday?" Olivia asked.

Everyone started talking at once. Emma had sold out of headbands. Stephanie would be busy baking all day just to fill the orders she'd taken. Olivia had fixed a load of appliances and a couple of computers, plus she'd been invited to help the local cycling club tune up their bikes. Mia had groomed more than a dozen pets – including the muddy poodle.

"How did you get on, Andrea?" Stephanie asked.

"I had a great time! I wish I could sing all day, every day." Andrea smiled at her friends. Then her smile faded slightly. "There's just one problem. Most people only put a few coins in the collection jar. It didn't add up to much money by the end of the day."

Mia looked worried. "We only have two more days before the mayor announces who's getting the tickets to the Piper Page concert."

Andrea bit her lip. "I know. I'll just have to keep singing and hope people are more generous with their donations."

"But what if you don't raise enough?" Now Olivia sounded worried, too. "You have to win a ticket!"

Emma nodded. "If you can't go, none of us should go."

"What?" Andrea couldn't believe her ears.

"But you guys are working so hard, and you all love Piper Page just as much as I do. If you win a place, you should go – no matter what happens to me."

But Olivia, Stephanie and Mia were all shaking their heads. "No way," Stephanie said. "Emma's right. It won't be any fun unless we're all there."

"All for one and one for all!" Mia shouted.

Olivia put an arm around Andrea. "You'd do the same for us, wouldn't you?"

Andrea hesitated, thinking about it for a moment. Would she pass up a chance to see Piper Page in concert if one of her friends couldn't go? She loved

Piper's music. And seeing her perform on a yacht was just about the coolest thing she could imagine.

Then she realized that Olivia was right. It wouldn't be any fun if all five of them weren't there enjoying it together.

"I'd definitely do the same for you guys," Andrea said, hugging Olivia back. "I guess this means I'll just have to figure out a way to raise more money for that charity so we all get to go – no matter what!"

A few minutes later, the five friends were walking into town. "Where are you going to put on your show today?" Emma asked Andrea.

"I asked Marie if I could sing at the café." Andrea smiled. "Most of my fans have seen me there, so maybe I'll raise more money."

"Good plan," Stephanie said. "I'm sure you'll make a lot of money for Page's Pets there!"

"I hope so." Andrea felt a twinge of worry. I hate the idea that my friends might miss the concert just because of me."

"All for one and one for all, remember?" Mia said. "Besides, there's no guarantee any of us will get tickets. We'll just have to wait and see."

"I guess you're right." Andrea squinted at the pavement up ahead. "Hey, isn't that Chelsea Noble?"

Chelsea had just stepped out of a flower shop holding a large shopping bag in each hand. Lots of colourful flowers were sticking out of the bags.

"Hey, Chelsea." Stephanie hurried over with her friends. "What's with all the flowers?"

Chelsea turned. "Oh, it's you guys," she said.
"Shouldn't you be out doing charity work?"

"We could ask you the same question." Andrea plucked a flower from one of Chelsea's bags and sniffed it. "These are pretty – I love roses."

"Give that back." Chelsea snatched the flower out of Andrea's hand. "These flowers are for my Piper Page fundraiser."

"What kind of fundraiser?" Andrea was surprised that Chelsea was actually doing charity work. Maybe she wasn't as lazy as they all thought.

"I'm throwing a tea party," Chelsea announced.

"A tea party?" Andrea exchanged a confused glance with her friends. "What do you mean? How do you raise money by throwing a tea party?"

"Easy," Chelsea said. "My parents go to parties that are fundraisers all the time. We host

the party and anyone who wants to come has
to make a donation to get in." She smiled.
"A big donation."

Mia looked sceptical. "Who are you going to
find to come to something like that? Most of
the kids at school can't afford to make a
big donation."

"I didn't invite anyone from school." Chelsea
rolled her eyes. "Some of mummy and daddy's
friends are coming."

Olivia frowned. "Why would adults come to
your tea party?"

"Yeah," Emma said. "Besides, do you even
know how to make tea?"

"I'm not making the tea myself, silly." Chelsea
laughed. "This is going to be a classy, professional
event. We've hired a catering company."

"But that's not fair!" Stephanie blurted out.

"Throwing a good party is a lot of work. I should know – I do it all the time. Are you doing any of the work yourself?"

Chelsea lifted her bags. "Of course. I'm picking up the flowers from the flower shop, aren't I?"

"That's not enough," Mia protested. "You're supposed to do actual charity work to raise the money, not just get your parents to convince their rich friends to donate."

"It doesn't say that," Chelsea smirked. "I checked the rules. My tea party definitely counts. And it's definitely going to get me a ticket to the yacht concert!"

Andrea frowned. It didn't seem fair that Chelsea was going to get a place on the yacht without doing any real charity work. Especially when Andrea and her friends were working so hard to earn their tickets.

Just then a large, shiny black car pulled up to the curb. "There's my ride." Chelsea picked up her bags of flowers again. "Cheerio girls! See you on the yacht – maybe."

8
And One For All

"Thank you, everyone! You've been a great audience!" Andrea grinned and waved.

There was a smattering of applause. The café was half empty.

Marie came over. "How's it going, Andrea?" the café owner asked.

"OK, I guess," Andrea said with a sigh. "I'm singing my heart out and I'm getting more donations than I did yesterday. I'm just not sure it's going to be enough."

Marie looked sympathetic. "The dinner crowd will be arriving soon. I'm sure you'll get more donations then."

"I hope so." Andrea glanced at the door, wishing the dinner crowd would hurry up and get there.

Instead, the door flew open and Stephanie rushed in. She was out of breath and grinning from ear to ear.

"Andrea!" she exclaimed, rushing over. "Guess what? I got you a gig!"

"A gig?" Andrea was confused. "What do you mean?"

Stephanie flopped into a chair to catch her breath. "This lady came by wanting to order cupcakes for her daughter's fifth birthday party tomorrow," she explained. "She mentioned that she'd hired a clown to entertain the children at the party. But he caught the flu and had to cancel."

"That's too bad." Andrea didn't get it. "But what does it have to do with me?"

Stephanie smiled. "I talked her into hiring you instead!"

"Me?" Andrea cried. "But I don't know how to clown around!"

"She's not hiring you to fall over," Stephanie explained. "I told her you're a fabulous singer, and that you know lots of childrens' songs."

Now Andrea understood. "So she wants to hire me to sing for the children at the party? Fun!"

Stephanie nodded. "Um, there's one more thing. I did tell her you'd wear a clown costume while you sing." She shrugged. "I know you won't look as cool as you do in your usual stage clothes, but she said her daughter really does love clowns. And she offered to double her donation to Page's Pets if you'd do it."

"I don't mind," Andrea grinned. "I'll wear anything she wants if it'll get me on Piper Page's yacht!" She grabbed Stephanie and hugged her. "Thanks so much!"

"You're welcome." Stephanie hugged her back. "All for one, and one for all!"

"OK, kids!" Andrea cried. "What song do you want to hear next?"

Nobody answered. Andrea wasn't sure anyone had even heard her, other than the birthday girl's mother.

"Sorry the kids are so noisy," she told Andrea with a smile. "All that sugar from the cupcakes must have made them a little excited."

"That's OK," Andrea said. "I'm glad they're having fun."

The fifth birthday party was in full swing, in

the back garden of one of the large, imposing houses near the harbour. The birthday girl and ten of her friends were playing games on the grass. Six little boys were screaming at the top of their voices as they chased one another around the swings. Some of the young

girls were picking bouquets from the flower beds. There were children sat at the picnic table and others were playing fetch with the dogs.

Andrea adjusted her clown wig. It was another warm, sunny afternoon, and she was hot inside her costume. But she didn't mind.

Happy Birthday!

She knew superstars like Piper Page performed in all kinds of weather and did their best. If they could do it, so could she!

She'd been singing children's songs and dancing in her clown costume since lunchtime. At times the children had listened or sung and danced along. But most of the time they seemed to forget she was there.

"You can take a break if you like, Andrea," the birthday girl's mother said. "It's hot out here and you've been singing non-stop for over an hour. You should probably rest your voice."

"Thanks, but I'm OK." The woman had given a huge donation to Page's Pets, and Andrea wanted to make sure she got her money's worth. She cleared her throat. "Hey, kids!" she tried again, raising her voice to be heard above the

noise. "Does anyone want to sing-along?" She
honked her red clown nose for attention.

A few little girls ran over, including the
birthday girl. "Sing more! Sing more!" one of
them cried.

"I'd love to." Andrea bent her knees and
leaned towards them with a smile. "What do
you want to hear?"

The little girls looked at one another
uncertainly. "Do you know any songs about
butterflies?" the birthday girl asked. "I love
butterflies."

"Um . . ." Andrea searched her mind for a
song about butterflies. She couldn't think of
any. "I don't think I know any songs about
butterflies.

But that doesn't mean
I can't make one up."

One of the other little girls looked impressed. "You can do that?"

"Of course!" Andrea smiled at her. "I write new songs all the time. It's fun!"

"Wow!" The birthday girl looked excited. "Sing the butterfly song!"

"OK." Andrea took a deep breath, focusing her mind on butterflies. She was a pretty good songwriter and she loved coming up with fun melodies and rhymes.

She started to sing, making up the words as she went along. The birthday girl loved it and she wasn't the only one. Soon every child at the party was listening.

"Yeah!" the birthday girl cheered when Andrea finished. "Make up another song!"

"OK!" said Andrea, looking pleased. She took a sip of water, then made up another song on the spot.

"Yay!" more children cheered when the song ended. "Do another one! Do another one!"

"Yeah," a children added. "Your songs are better than normal songs!"

Andrea smiled. She was glad Stephanie had found this gig for her. And not just because it meant she might get to see Piper Page. She was having a great time!

"Thanks!" she said, taking a bow. "What should my next song be about?"

9
Lost For Words

The next morning, Andrea hurried to the tree
house. The five girls were meeting to listen
to the mayor on the radio. He was going to
announce who had won tickets to Piper's
concert!

When she arrived, her friends were already
there. "Finally!" Stephanie cried when she saw
Andrea's head poke up over the edge of the
tree house. "We were afraid you wouldn't make
it in time."

"Here I am," Andrea said.

At least that was what she meant to say. But
all that came out was a hoarse croak.

Mia blinked at her. "Are you OK?"

Andrea cleared her throat and tried again. "I'm fine," she said.

At least that was what she meant to say. Once again, all that came out was a croak.

"Uh, oh," Olivia said. "It sounds like you lost your voice! That happened to me once after I went to see a football match with my dad and cheered too much."

"It happened to me when I had the flu last year," Emma said. "Try whispering instead of talking. Sometimes that works better."

"How's this?" Andrea whispered. This time the words came out OK – just quiet.

Olivia leaned forward. "So what happened to your voice?"

"I'm not sure," Andrea whispered. "It was OK at the party, but my throat started feeling a little tired at the end."

"Oh, right." Emma brightened. "Steph told us about the party. How did it go?"

"Fantastic!" Andrea tried to shout. When she heard her croaking voice, she remembered to whisper. "Fantastic," she whispered. "The children loved all of my songs. Especially the ones I made up just for them!"

"That sounds great," Stephanie said. "I knew you'd be a big hit!"

"So you spent all day singing songs to a group of noisy children?" Mia smiled. "No wonder you lost your voice."

"Shh!" Olivia was leaning closer to the radio. "The mayor's coming on now."

They all gathered around as Olivia turned up the volume. The mayor read out the names of the winners... and the girls were delighted to discover they'd all won tickets – including Andrea!

"Hooray!" she shouted.

Or she tried to, anyway. All that came out was another croak.

Stephanie frowned. "How long do you think it'll take for your voice to come back?" she asked. "Will you be OK in time to sing with Piper Page tomorrow?"

Andrea hadn't thought about that. "I hope so," she whispered.

But the next morning, Andrea's voice still hadn't returned. She walked glumly to the harbour, trying to cheer herself up with thoughts of the concert on the yacht. A huge crowd had gathered by the pier. Andrea spotted her friends and hurried over.

Olivia looked stunning in a pink minidress, Emma was super-stylish in a black skirt and sparkly camisole, Stephanie's blue dress set off her blue eyes and Mia had traded in her practical trousers for a flippy lavender skirt and pale green top.

"You look great, Andrea," Emma said.

"Thanks." Andrea whispered, glancing down at her dress. "I heard green is Piper's favourite colour."

"Wow." Olivia looked around. "There are a lot of people here."

"Yeah," Mia agreed. "A lot more than twenty-five, that's for sure."

Andrea stared at the enormous white yacht moored close to the pier. It was sparkling white

Charity Concert

with shiny golden rails – just as big and fancy
as Chelsea had told them.

Stephanie pointed to a sign near the pier.
"Look, it says we should sign in for the concert
over there."

The girls hurried over and gave their names
to a tense-looking woman with a clipboard.
"All right, you're all checked off," she said,
making a mark on her clipboard. "You can go
in and wait with the others through there."

She unhooked a red velvet rope from a post.
A smaller group of people was milling around
on the other side. Chelsea was one of them.

"Hi, Chelsea," Emma said, leading the others
over. "This is cool, isn't it?"

"It sure is." Olivia hugged herself with
excitement. "I can't believe we're about to see
Piper Page sing live!"

"I can't wait," Chelsea said. "I'm going to make sure I'm right at the front when Piper's assistant comes around with the microphone. I want to make sure Piper hears my singing voice. I bet she'll love it. She might even want me to record a song with her!"

Andrea didn't say anything. She was still excited to see Piper Page perform. But Chelsea's words reminded her that she wouldn't get a chance to sing along on 'Friends Forever.'

Had losing her voice messed up Andrea's chance to make her dreams come true?

10
Piper's Concert

A few minutes later, a young man stepped onto the yacht's gangplank.

"Hello, everyone," he said in a loud, cheerful voice. "I'm Rocky, Piper's assistant. Welcome to the yacht concert!"

Everyone cheered. Andrea couldn't make any noise, so she waved both hands over her head instead. Her heart thumped with excitement and she forgot all about her missing voice. She was about to see her idol!

Rocky ushered the charity winners onto the yacht. It was even posher inside than outside.

The girls and the other winners walked down
a plush hallway lined with gold albums and
pictures of Piper looking gorgeous. Then
Rocky led them out onto a large wooden
deck strung with fairy lights. A stage was set up
at one end. A few people were rushing around
setting up leads and speakers.

"Wow," Emma said. "This is so cool!"

Mia looked around. "Where's Olivia?"

"I think she stopped when we passed the
engine room," Stephanie said. "She wanted to
see if she could find out more about how the
ship works."

Emma laughed. "Typical Olivia!"

A moment later Olivia arrived. "This yacht
is really great," she told her friends. "The radar
system is super advanced!"

"Forget about the radar," Stephanie

said with a grin, throwing an arm around Olivia's shoulders. "It's time to have fun with Piper Page!"

Andrea grinned. She was still disappointed that she'd lost her voice. But she was going to have fun anyway.

"Do you feel that?" Emma said.

"Feel what?" Olivia asked, watching as a couple of guys pushed a large drum kit out onto the stage.

"I think we're leaving the shore," Mia said.

Mia was right. Andrea could feel the yacht's powerful engines making the whole deck vibrate.

"Let's go and wave to the people back on shore," Stephanie said.

The five girls rushed to the rail. The yacht was pulling out into the harbour. Andrea and her friends waved to the crowd still gathered by

the pier. The crowd
cheered and
waved back.

"Say hi to Piper
for us!" a man yelled.

"We will!" Stephanie
called back.

Soon the yacht
was chugging along
the shore towards
Ambersands Beach.
The beautiful skyline
of Heartlake City was
spread out above a sparkling blue sea Andrea
admired the view for a moment. Then she poked
Olivia on the arm and leaned towards her.

"Let's find a spot closer to the stage,"
Andrea whispered.

"Good idea." Olivia glanced at the others. "Andrea says let's move closer. We want to be able to see and hear everything!"

The five of them hurried across the deck. Chelsea followed.

"This looks like a good spot," Chelsea said, pushing between Andrea and Mia to get right in front of the stage. "Rocky will definitely see me here when it's time for a fan to sing."

Mia looked at Andrea and rolled her eyes. Andrea just shrugged, feeling sad again for a second. She wished she could have a chance to sing for Piper.

Then the lights around the stage flashed on. They were every colour of the rainbow and the stage looked like a beautiful birthday cake, all lit up! Andrea's heart leapt. At the same time, the band ran out from backstage. They

carried guitars, tambourines and keyboards. One woman was carrying a pair of drumsticks; she slid in behind the drum kit.

"Look!" Emma jumped up and down. "That's Piper's band!"

The girls and the rest of the audience cheered. Andrea wished she could join in. Then she remembered another way she could make herself heard. She stuck two fingers in her mouth and let out a loud whistle.

"Hey," Chelsea complained. "You whistled right in my ear!"

Andrea ignored her. Piper Page herself had just stepped onstage!

"Piper! Piper!" Stephanie and Olivia chanted.

"Hello, everyone!" Piper called out, waving to the crowd as she walked to the front of the stage. She was wearing a glittering gold dress

that sparkled as brightly as her yacht. Her hair was piled on top of her head and studded with diamonds. She looked like a glorious shining star! "Thanks for coming today. And thanks for raising so much money to help homeless animals!"

"Yay!" Mia cheered, clapping her hands.

Soon the show started. The first song was
a popular one called 'Up in the Air'. Andrea
could hardly believe she was really watching
Piper Page perform in the middle of Heartlake
Harbor. It was amazing!

Piper performed one hit after another, and Andrea and her friends danced along happily, laughing and waving their arms in the air.

"Ready for another one?" Piper said into the microphone.

The guitarist strummed a chord. "Listen!" Emma shrieked, grabbing Andrea's arm. "It's 'Friends Forever!'"

She was right. The familiar opening music was pouring out of the speakers. "We were strangers when we met," Piper sang. "Now we're close as friends can get . . ."

Andrea wished she could sing along. She knew every word to 'Friends Forever!' Instead she danced and listened to her friends sing along with Piper.

Soon Rocky appeared at the edge of the stage. He was holding a golden microphone.

"Over here! Over here!" Chelsea waved her hands and jumped up and down.

Rocky didn't notice her. Instead, he walked over and handed the microphone to a tiny, dark-haired girl on the opposite side of the stage. She gasped, then grabbed it.

"We're friends forever, friends forever," she sang loudly. "Stuck like glue, me and you!"

Her voice was squeaky and nervous. But Andrea could see that she was having fun. Then Rocky pulled the microphone away and handed it to a tall, red-haired boy standing nearby. He sang the next couple of lines, looking excited.

When the chorus ended, the audience members who'd got the chance to sing were hugged and cheered by their friends. Andrea smiled as she watched them, but she felt a

little bit sad. One of those singers could have been her! If only she hadn't overdone it at the birthday party and lost her voice.

Chelsea was frowning. "That's not fair," she said. "I didn't get a chance to sing!"

"I think Rocky's coming this way," Emma said, pointing at the assistant who was now pushing through the crowd in their direction.

He reached them just as Piper got ready to sing the chorus again. As soon as Rocky held up the microphone, Chelsea jumped forward

and grabbed it out of his hand. "We're friends forever, friends foooor-ev-errrr!" she sang.

Andrea winced. Chelsea hadn't sounded too bad at the café. Today she

sounded terrible! She was off-key and ahead of the music.

After two or three lines, Rocky tried to take the microphone back. But Chelsea yanked it away, still singing.

"Hey," Mia complained. "Let someone else have a go!"

Finally Rocky wrestled the microphone away from Chelsea. "Who's next?" he said. He held the microphone towards Andrea. "Would you like to try?"

All Andrea could do was shake her head. Rocky shrugged and turned to the others. Chelsea started to reach for the microphone again.

"I'll do it," Stephanie said, shooting Andrea a worried

look. She took the microphone and sang the last few lines of the chorus along with Piper.

When she finished, her friends cheered. "Good job, Steph," Olivia said.

Andrea knew Stephanie wouldn't be able to hear her whispers over the music. So she just grabbed her and hugged her. "Brilliant!" she mouthed.

"Thanks." Stephanie smiled and hugged her back. "I wish it was you, though."

Me too, Andrea thought sadly.

Then she shook off the thought. This was a once-in-a-lifetime chance to see a fabulous concert by her favourite singer. She didn't want to waste it worrying about what might have been.

11
A Super Surprise

"That was amazing!" Stephanie squealed, jumping up and down. "I still can't believe we just saw Piper Page in concert."

"I know!" Mia exclaimed. "She sang all her best songs."

The concert had ended, and the five girls were walking off the yacht with the rest of the audience. They made their way along the pier as the sun set along the water's edge. Lots of people were strolling along with them, or going to and from the other boats moored nearby. Most of them stared curiously at the girls and the other concert-goers.

Emma's eyes sparkled. "I loved it when she sang 'Dance Party,'" she said. "I think that was the best one. Or wait – 'Up in the Air' sounded really good, too. So did 'My Secret.' And of course 'Friends Forever' is always good . . ."

Olivia giggled. "Just admit it – they all sounded great."

"You're right," Emma shrugged, running her hands through her dark hair. "I admit it!"

Andrea laughed, even though no sound came out. Her heart was still racing from the excitement of the concert. It had been just as incredible as she'd expected. Well, except for one part . . .

She tried not to think about that. In all her daydreams, she'd imagined taking the microphone and belting out the chorus of 'Friends Forever' along with Piper.

She'd pictured the superstar smiling at her, maybe saying how great she sounded. Maybe even asking if Andrea wanted to come up on stage and sing another song with her.

But none of that had happened. Andrea had missed her chance.

"What time is it?" Olivia asked. "I told my dad to pick us up at five."

Emma checked her stylish silver watch. "We're about ten minutes early."

"Let's sit down while we wait," Stephanie suggested. "My legs are about to fall off from dancing so much."

"Mine, too," Mia said.

There were some benches near the main road leading into the city. The girls flopped onto the seats, exhausted. Andrea stood to one side.

"There's room to sit with us, Andrea," Olivia said, patting the bench between her and Emma.

Andrea smiled but shook her head. She didn't feel like sitting down. She was still too hyped up from the show. It might have been the most exciting day of her whole life. If only she could have sung when Rocky had offered her the microphone. Then it would have been absolutely perfect!

For a moment she wished she hadn't taken the singing clown job. Then her voice would still be OK.

Almost immediately, she shook her head. It was silly to think that way. For one thing, if she hadn't taken that job, she probably wouldn't have won a place on the yacht. More importantly, she wouldn't have raised as much money for the charity. And most

importantly, she still smiled when she
remembered how excited the children had
been to hear her sing. She wouldn't trade that
for anything – not even the chance to sing for
Piper Page.

But still . . . she did wish she could have
done both . . .

Andrea heard hurried footsteps and turned
to find Chelsea running towards them.

The others turned, too. "Wasn't that a great
concert, Chelsea?" Olivia asked politely.

"Definitely," Chelsea agreed. "Would you
guys like my autograph?"

Mia stared at her. "Your autograph? Why
would we want that?"

Chelsea tossed her hair. "You heard me
during 'Friends Forever,' right?" she said.
"I sounded fantastic. I'm sure Piper Page will

be contacting me soon to see if I want to sing with her again."

"If you say so." Emma sounded dubious.

"Friends forever, friends forever!" Chelsea sang loudly.

A woman paused to stare at her. Chelsea smiled.

"Would you like my autograph?" she asked the woman. "I'll be famous soon."

"Thanks, but I'm in a hurry." The woman rushed off.

Andrea saw her friends sharing

amused looks. But she wasn't in the mood to laugh, even though Chelsea was being pretty silly. All Andrea could think about was Rocky holding out the microphone – and knowing that she couldn't take it. She'd missed her big chance to sing for her idol. What if that was the only opportunity she'd ever get to make it big?

Chelsea finished singing and peered down the street. "My limo should be here soon," she announced. "It's a good thing I'm already used to riding around in swanky cars, since that's how all the superstar singers get around."

Andrea was getting tired of listening to Chelsea brag. It just reminded her of how much she'd wanted to sing for Piper.

"Look, that must be your limo coming now," Emma said. She pointed to a long, black car with tinted windows. It was rolling slowly

along the street towards them.

Chelsea leaned out for a better look. "Actually, that doesn't look like my dad's limo. His is bigger."

"Are you sure?" Mia said. "Because it looks like it's stopping."

Sure enough, the limousine pulled up to the curb right in front of the girls. The rear window rolled down.

Andrea gasped. It was Piper Page, taking off her sunglasses and smiling!

"Piper!" Stephanie shrieked. "Is that really you?"

Olivia was wide-eyed. "But – but we just saw you sing!" she blurted out. Piper smiled at the girls. "Thanks for coming to my concert,"

she said. "And for all the hard work you guys did for my charity."

"You're welcome, Piper." Chelsea elbowed the others out of the way to get to the car window. "It's me, Chelsea! I'm the one who sang 'Friends Forever' with you, remember?"

"Sure," Piper said. "You sounded great."

"Thanks, Piper." Chelsea shot Andrea and her friends a smug look.

Andrea felt her heart sink. Could Chelsea be right? Had she impressed Piper Page with her singing? Was that why Piper had stopped when she saw them?

But Piper was peering past Chelsea at the other girls. "Is one of you called Andrea?" she asked.

12

Friends Forever

Andrea gasped. Was she hearing things? Or had Piper Page really just said her name?

"That's me!" she cried, but all that came out of her mouth was a weak croak.

"This is Andrea," Stephanie spoke up quickly, shoving Andrea forward. "She's your biggest fan. She can't talk right now, though — she lost her voice by singing her heart out for your charity."

"Yes, I heard about her singing." Piper smiled at Andrea and held out her hand. "Nice to meet you, Andrea. I hear you have quite a voice."

Andrea shook Piper's hand. She would have been too stunned to speak – even if she hadn't lost her voice. How did Piper know her name? How did she know she was a singer? The questions raced through Andrea's mind. But she couldn't ask any of them without her voice!

Luckily, her friends came to the rescue again. "How did you hear about Andrea?" Emma asked eagerly. "I mean, she's pretty famous here in Heartlake City, but we didn't know she was world famous."

Piper chuckled. "She isn't world famous yet," she said. "But from what I hear, she might be soon!"

"What do you mean?" Chelsea sounded surprised and a little annoyed.

"My older sister still lives here in Heartlake City," Piper explained. "One of her daughter's friends had a birthday party yesterday, and my sister and niece were there. They both told me the singing clown at the party was fantastic."

"That was Andrea!" Stephanie cried, jumping up and down. "She was the singing clown!"

Piper laughed. "I know. My sister even

recorded some of her songs on her mobile phone. She played them back for me last night, and I was really impressed."

Andrea could hardly believe her ears. "Thank you," she whispered.

"She sang all day long," Olivia told Piper. "That's how she lost her voice."

"I never lose my voice!" Chelsea shouted, pushing her way to the front of the group again. "That's important if I want to be a singer, isn't it?"

"Andrea only lost her voice because she was working so hard to raise money for the charity," Mia told Chelsea with a frown.

"Yes, it happens to most singers at some point,"

Piper said. "It even happened to me once."

"Really?" Emma sounded amazed. "You lost your voice, Piper?"

"That's terrible!" Stephanie exclaimed. Then she gave Andrea an apologetic look. "I mean, it's terrible it happened to you, too, Andrea. But it's extra terrible that it happened to Piper Page!"

Andrea smiled. She knew what Stephanie meant. "What happened?" she whispered to Piper.

"I was in a big hurry to finish recording my second album," Piper said. "I stayed in the studio day and night. I finished early, but I also ended up straining my voice so badly that I couldn't talk at all. The worst part is, I was meant to perform on a TV show two days later. It was terrible!"

"What happened?" Olivia asked. "Did you get your voice back in time?"

"No," Piper said. "Luckily they let me come back after I recovered. But after that, I learned to take better care of my voice."

Andrea nodded. She'd learned her lesson, too!

"If Andrea could talk, I'm sure she'd say she was happy you liked her singing," Stephanie said.

Andrea nodded. That was exactly what she would have said.

Piper smiled. "I mean it – I loved your voice, and also the songs you made up for the children," she told Andrea. "You're very creative! In fact, I'm doing a special version of 'Friends Forever' as a charity single for Page's Pets. I'd love it if you could help me adjust the lyrics – and then record the song with me."

Andrea and all her friends gasped. "Really?" Emma exclaimed. "You want Andrea to sing with you?"

Chelsea looked angry. "Are you sure you want her to record with you?"

"Definitely," Piper smiled. "What do you say, Andrea?"

Andrea was grinning so hard her jaw started hurting! She wanted to scream "Yes!" but instead she nodded and gave Piper a double thumbs-up.

"Ready?" Piper Page looked over at Andrea and smiled.

"Ready!" Andrea said clearly into the microphone.

It was a week after the concert and her voice was good as new. Piper Page and Andrea were in a professional recording studio in downtown Heartlake City. Andrea's friends were watching through a big glass window. The studio crew

were setting the sound on the mixer and adjusting the microphones.

Finally, one of them pointed to Andrea and Piper. "Go!" he mouthed.

The background music started. Andrea smiled and swayed to the beat.

Soon Piper came in, right on cue:

"We were strangers when we met," she sang.

Next it was Andrea's turn: "Now you're my super special pet . . ."

They continued the song, changing a few words so it was about being friends with animals. Finally they reached the chorus:

"We're friends forever; skin, fur, or feather
We're stuck like glue, me and you –
My animal friends are forever true."

Andrea was grinning from ear to ear. Outside the window, she could see her friends dancing and singing along. She waved to them as Piper sang the second-to-last line of the song.

Then it was Andrea's turn again. She focused on the microphone, putting everything she had

into her last line. She let her voice really ring out on the last word: "For-evvvv-errrrr!"

Because that was how long Andrea would remember this extra special day!

THE END

Andrea
Star Performer

Hair colour:
Dark brown.

Style:
Andrea wears funky, colourful clothes that are easy to dance in and look great on stage!

Loves:
Writing and composing songs, dancing, working at the Heartlake City Café.

Favourite animal:
Her white rabbit, Jazz.

Her friends sometimes think she's . . . :
A bit of a drama queen! But she's just the type of girl exciting things happen to!

Dream:
To be a famous singer and perform with Piper Page!

Olivia
Brilliant Inventor

Hair colour:
Chestnut.

Style:
Although she often wears a lab coat, Olivia has great style and is famous for her stylish hair accessories.

Loves:
Science, inventing things, exploring the natural world.

Favourite animals:
Her cat, Kitty, her dog, Scarlett and her foal, Snow.

Her friends sometimes think she's . . . :
Stubborn – but only because she's usually right!

Dream:
To become a famous scientist or engineer.

Stephanie
Social Butterfly

Hair colour:
Blonde.

Style:
Stephanie loves pink! She especially likes to match her accessories with her outfits – right down to her pink mobile phone!

Loves:
Planning events, playing football, baking.

Favourite animals:
Her bunny, Daisy and her dog, Coco.

Her friends sometimes think she's . . . :
A bit bossy . . . but she just wants to make sure everything is perfect!

Dream:
To become a journalist or party planner.

Emma
Stylish Designer

Hair colour:
Black.

Style:
Emma is always up to date with
all the latest fashions. Like a true designer,
she makes a lot of her own fabulous clothes!

Loves:
Designing clothes and jewellery,
photography, martial arts.

Favourite animal:
Her horse, Robin.

Her friends sometimes think she's . . . :
Forgetful, but she never forgets to accessorize!

Dream:
To become a fashion designer.

Mia
Animal Lover

Hair colour:
Red.

Style:
Mia is a practical girl and likes
simple trousers and t-shirts . . .
and she loves anything with an animal on it!

Loves:
Looking after animals, playing the drums,
magic tricks.

Favourite animals:
Her dog, Charlie, her horse, Bella.

Her friends sometimes think she's . . . :
A bit of a pushover . . . but she just really likes
helping people!

Dream:
To be a vet, animal psychologist or run
a pet rescue centre.

Which LEGO® Friend are you?

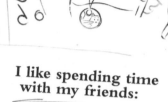

I would never:

- (D) Say no to karaoke!
- (A) Squash an insect
- (E) Leave home without a handbag!
- (C) Miss my friends' birthdays
- (B) Fail a maths test

My favourite accessory is:

- (E) Funky jewellery
- (B) A practical bag with lots of pockets
- (A) A rucksack
- (D) A brocade belt
- (C) A colourful watch

My favourite sport is:

- (E) Martial arts
- (D) Dancing
- (A) Horse riding
- (B) Hiking
- (C) Football

I like spending time with my friends:

- (E) In the shopping centre
- (D) At a concert
- (B) In a tree house
- (A) In the park
- (C) At a party

I'm good at:

- (C) Organizing things
- (D) Singing
- (B) Taking photos
- (A) Looking after animals
- (E) Drawing

A You are like Mia. Both of you love animals and nature. Keeping clothes simple helps you feel comfortable during your favourite outdoor activities.

B You are like Olivia. You're inventive, clever and good at science. You love hanging out with your best friends at a secret hideout!

C You're just like Stephanie. You both love a party, especially if you've organized it! You're fun, chatty and sociable and people love being around you.

D You and Andrea are like two peas in a pod. Dancing and singing is your passion. In your free time, you love cooking and eating delicious food!

E You and Emma have a lot in common. You both like fashion and wouldn't leave home in clothes and accessories that don't match! You're also sporty and great at martial arts.

Summer Sleepover Party

Summer sleepovers are so much fun! Read Stephanie's tips for throwing the perfect party and have your own fantastic sleepover, just like the girls.

Prepare some snacks – Yummy things like popcorn or muffins are great for a sweet treat, but remember to include some healthier snacks and drinks, such as crunchy vegetables and fruit juice.

Karaoke – Andrea loves karaoke – and it's a great group activity! Try splitting into teams, practising a song and performing it for each other!

Truth or Dare – Party games are a must for your sleepover. Take it in turns to choose a 'truth' or a 'dare' – either answer a question, or perform a dare!

Foil Make Over Game – Emma loves this stylish activity! Ask your parents to get a few rolls of aluminium foil, then crunch and shape it into fabulous outfits and do a fashion show!

Spooky stories – Once it's dark, try Olivia's favourite pastime: telling ghost stories! Use a torch to light up your face and use a scary voice to tell your tale.

"Friends Forever"
by Piper Page

We were strangers when we met,
Now we're close as friends can get.
We can make all dreams come true,
Cause we're best friends, me and you.

We're friends forever, friends forever –
We're stuck like glue, me and you.
Friends, friends, friends, forever true!

We can have the greatest fun,
We can make a secret plan,
Each time you can count on me,
This is how it'll always be.

We're friends forever, friends forever . . .